INSTRUMENTAL PLAY-ALONG

CHRISTMAS FAVOURITES

Contents

TITLE	PAGE	CD TRACK
Blue Christmas	2	1
Caroling, Caroling	3	2
Feliz Navidad	4	3
Frosty The Snowman	5	4
Happy Xmas (War Is Over)	6	5
Here Comes Santa Claus (Right Down Santa Claus Lane)	7	6
(There's No Place Like) Home For The Holidays	8	7
It's Beginning To Look Like Christmas	9	8
Jingle Bell Rock	10	9
Let It Snow! Let It Snow! Let It Snow!	11	10
Little Saint Nick	12	11
Merry Christmas, Darling	13	12
My Favourite Things	14	13
Santa Baby	15	14
Silver Bells	16	15
B♭ Tuning Notes		16

HOW TO USE THE CD ACCOMPANIMENT:
A melody cue appears on the right channel only. If your CD player has a balance adjustm
of the melody by turning down the right channel.

GW00400999

This publication is not authorised for sale in the United States of America

Exclusive Distributors:
Music Sales Limited
14-15 Berners Street, London W1T 3LJ, UK.

Order No. HLE90003255
ISBN: 978-1-84772-313-0
This book © Copyright 2007 Hal Leonard Europe

Printed in the USA

Your Guarantee of Quality
As publishers, we strive to produce every book to the highest commercial standards. The book has been carefully designed to minimise awkward page turns and to make playing from it a real pleasure. Throughout, the printing and binding have been planned to ensure a sturdy, attractive publication which should give years of enjoyment. If your copy fails to meet our high standards, please inform us and we will gladly replace it.

www.musicsales.com

HLE
HAL LEONARD EUROPE
DISTRIBUTED BY MUSIC SALES

◆ BLUE CHRISTMAS

FLUTE

Words and Music by BILLY HAYES
and JAY JOHNSON

❷ CAROLING, CAROLING

Flute

Words by WIHLA HUTSON
Music by ALFRED BURT

❸ FELIZ NAVIDAD

FLUTE

Music and Lyrics by
JOSÉ FELICIANO

◆ FROSTY THE SNOWMAN

Words and Music by
STEVE NELSON and JACK ROLLINS

Flute

♦5 HAPPY XMAS
(War Is Over)

FLUTE

Words and Music by JOHN LENNON
and YOKO ONO

⬥6 HERE COMES SANTA CLAUS
(Right Down Santa Claus Lane)

FLUTE

Words and Music by GENE AUTRY
and OAKLEY HALDEMAN

(There's No Place Like)
HOME FOR THE HOLIDAYS

FLUTE

Words by AL STILLMAN
Music by ROBERT ALLEN

❽ ◆ IT'S BEGINNING TO LOOK LIKE CHRISTMAS

FLUTE

By MEREDITH WILLSON

◆⑨ JINGLE BELL ROCK

Words and Music by
JOE BEAL and JIM BOOTHE

FLUTE

◆⑩ LET IT SNOW! LET IT SNOW! LET IT SNOW!

Words by SAMMY CAHN
Music by JULE STYNE

Flute

♦11 LITTLE SAINT NICK

Flute

Words and Music by BRIAN WILSON
and MIKE LOVE

⑫ MERRY CHRISTMAS, DARLING

Flute

Words and Music by RICHARD CARPENTER
and FRANK POOLER

MY FAVOURITE THINGS

From THE SOUND OF MUSIC

Lyrics by OSCAR HAMMERSTEIN II
Music by RICHARD RODGERS

FLUTE

SANTA BABY

Flute

By JOAN JAVITS,
PHIL SPRINGER and TONY SPRINGER

🎵 SILVER BELLS

From the Paramount Motion Picture THE LEMON DROP KID

Words and Music by
JAY LIVINGSTON and RAY EVANS

FLUTE